THE SIEGE OF
FRIMLY PRIM

THE SIEGE OF FRIMLY PRIM

Robert Swindells

Illustrated by Scoular Anderson

MAMMOTH

First published in Great Britain 1993
by Methuen Children's Books Ltd
Published 1994 by Mammoth
an imprint of Reed Books Ltd
Michelin House, 81 Fulham Road, London SW3 6RB
and Auckland, Melbourne, Singapore and Toronto

Reprinted 1995, 1996

ISBN 0 7497 1780 7

A CIP catalogue record for this title
is available from the British Library

Printed and bound in Great Britain
by Cox & Wyman Ltd, Reading, Berkshire

Contents

1	Wild Rumours	7
2	You'd End Up in Jail	11
3	A Rotten Shame	17
4	Killing a Pig	22
5	Plan of Action	29
6	Easy	37
7	A Box of Chalks	44
8	Hass-Cream	51
9	Goodies and Baddies	58
10	Getting Cold	63
11	New Hostage	66
12	Teddy Bears	74
13	The Right Thing	86
14	Three Cheers	93

CHAPTER ONE

Wild Rumours

'Closing the school?' Rory frowned at Sally. 'How d'you mean? Who? How can they – it's the only one we've got.'

The girl shrugged. 'Don't ask me. My mum got it from one of the old folks down the cottages. Mrs Hassett, I think.'

'Mrs Hassett?' Rory laughed. 'She's Stanton's gran, Skeeter.' Skeeter was Sally's nickname. 'You know what a load of rubbish The Hass talks.' Stanton, the most unpopular boy in the school, was known to everybody as The Hass. 'His gran's probably the same. Runs in the family.'

'Yes,' said Skeeter, 'but The Hass's dad's Chairman of the School Governors so he'd know, and old Mrs Hassett's his mother, right?'

Rory grinned wryly. 'And you think he'd tell his mother before he told Golly?' Golly was the Head Teacher. His real name was Mr Robertson.

'He might. And anyway, how d'you know he hasn't told Golly?'

Rory shook his head. 'If Golly knew, we'd know. He'd have announced it in assembly or something. No, Skeeter. It's a rumour. A tale. A load of old rubbish. Come on – I want to call in at Ward's for some crisps before the bell goes.'

Cheryl stuck her head through the bead curtain which separated the house from the shop. 'I'm off now, Mum.'

'Right, love.' Mrs Ward was building a pyramid from tins of tuna. 'Got your lunch?'

'Yes, Mum.'

'Tissues?'

Cheryl sighed. 'Yes, Mum, I've got everything. See you at tea-time.'

She let herself out through the house door. Her dad was stacking crates in the yard. 'Have a nice day, love,' he said.

'Thanks, Dad. You too.' Nice day. Fat chance when you're going to spend it at school. She was closing the gate when Rory called to her.

'Hey, Cher – your mum got any free crisps today?'

''Fraid not, Smudge.' Rory's name was Smith, but his friends always called him Smudge. 'Last packet went ten minutes ago.'

'Just my rotten luck. I'll have to pay then. Hang on a minute and we'll walk on together.'

The bell pinged as he opened the shop door. Skeeter said, 'Hey, Cher, you'll never guess.'

'What?' Skeeter always seemed to have a story to tell. Some news. A secret. She was forever saying, 'you'll never guess'.

She told Cheryl about the school. 'Smudge reckons it's rubbish but I don't, do you?'

Cheryl shrugged. 'Dunno. You hear about schools closing. It's on the news a lot, but ours is the only one in Frimly. I can't see 'em closing it. Where would we go?'

'Bannerfield, I expect. There's loads of schools in Bannerfield.'

'Bannerfield's nine miles!'

The bell pinged again as Smudge emerged in time to hear Cheryl's exclamation. He grinned. 'Take no notice of Skeeter, Cher. She's spreading wild rumours as usual.' He crammed two crackling packets into his sports bag and swung it over his shoulder. 'Come on, or they'll have shut down before we get there.'

CHAPTER TWO

You'd End Up in Jail

As soon as Smudge saw Golly's face he knew something was wrong. They'd had the hymn and the prayer and now it was time for the notices. Today was Monday, and Monday's notices were usually about swimming certificates or how the school football team got on last Saturday or some jumble sale the parents were planning. Golly nearly always looked cheerful on Monday morning because he believed in starting the week with a smile, but today he looked grave. 'Children,' he said, 'this morning is not a happy one for Frimly Primary School.'

Smudge nudged Cher and whispered, 'I bet the football team lost sixty-eight–nil.'

Cher shook her head. 'It's worse than that, Smudge. I can tell by his face.'

'Last Friday evening,' the Head continued, 'there was a meeting between the School Governors and representatives of the

Education Department.' He paused, gazing down at the children. 'The department feels that there are no longer enough children in our school, and so it will close at the end of this term.' A gasp arose from the startled pupils. Skeeter looked at Smudge and mouthed, 'Told you!' Smudge stuck his tongue out at her. Mrs Ball, the infants' teacher, smiled bravely in her place by the wall.

'After Christmas,' said Golly, 'each of you will begin to attend the school of your parents' choice in Bannerfield.'

So, mused Smudge, as the Head dismissed the assembly, old Skeeter was right for once. What a shame. Not that I'm crazy about school or anything, but Frimly Prim's certainly better than travelling nine miles to Bannerfield every day. I'd get saddled with Jilly and she's a total nuisance. (Jilly was Smudge's sister. She was seven, and she and Smudge couldn't stand each other. They never walked to school together but he knew they'd have to catch the same bus into Bannerfield.) I don't fancy that at all, and I bet nobody else does either. Surely there's something we can do about it?

He didn't get much work done first lesson. His brain was busy with other things.

'I think we should have a march,' Smudge said. It was break-time. Cher and Skeeter were sharing his crisps in a corner of the yard.

The girls looked at him. 'What are you on about, Smudge?' demanded Cher. 'What sort of march? What for?'

'A protest march,' said Smudge. 'To stop 'em closing the school.'

'Where would we march to, and how would it stop 'em closing the school?'

Smudge sighed. 'We'd march to the whatsit, of course – the Education Department. All of us. Just think how worried they'd get surrounded by hundreds of shouting kids.'

Skeeter laughed. 'There's only thirty-one kids in the whole school, Smudge. I don't think they'd be all that worried. Anyway, I've got a better idea.'

'Go on, then, clever-clogs – what's your idea?'

'Occupy the school,' said Skeeter. Smudge looked at her.

'What does occupy mean?'

'It means we barricade ourselves inside the school and refuse to come out. They did it at this hospital my mum used to work at. It was going to close, so the doctors and nurses locked themselves inside and just stayed there.'

'And what happened?'

'They kept it going a whole year. It was on telly and everything. It closed down in the end, but at least they made a fight of it.'

'Hmm.' Smudge looked dubious. 'I dunno.'

'Just because you didn't think of it,' said Cher. 'I think it's a brill idea, Skeeter.'

'What's a brill idea?' Matthew Pinkney had overheard. 'What are you lot whispering about?'

'Not a lot, Pinko,' said Cher. 'Only taking over the school.'

'Oh, yeah, I'll bet. You and whose army?'

'It's right, Pinko,' Skeeter told him. 'That's what we're talking about.'

'You're crazy.'

'No. we're not. We're talking about saving our school. Would you join us if we did it?'

'No way!' Pinko shook his head. 'You'd end up in jail. And anyway, you won't do it.'

'Don't you be too sure,' growled Smudge. The girls looked at him. 'I thought you didn't fancy the idea,' said Skeeter.

'Yeah, well.' Smudge shrugged. He didn't like Pinko much. If Matthew Pinkney was daring him to do something, he might do it just to show him. 'What we need is a meeting. All the juniors. Somewhere quiet, after school.'

'The quarry?' suggested Cher. There was a long-abandoned quarry at the end of the village. Grown-ups never went there so it was a good place to mess about in.

Smudge nodded. 'OK – the quarry. Tell everybody except The Hass. We don't want him carrying tales to his daddy or this thing'll be over before it even starts.'

CHAPTER THREE

A Rotten Shame

It was drizzling when Smudge and Skeeter reached the quarry, but the juniors were there. All fourteen of them. Stanton Hassett was missing, but that was how they'd planned it. There was some muttering as the two friends appeared.

'Come on, Smudge, it's chucking it down.'

'Yeah, we're stuck here drowning while you stroll along with your girlfriend, taking your time.'

Smudge flushed. 'She's not my girlfriend, you div, but she's got an idea and we wanted you all to hear it.'

'Well, come on then – we'll be missing *Neighbours* at this rate.'

Briefly, Skeeter told them about her idea. When she'd finished, everybody started talking at once. Smudge picked up a stick and banged it on a rock to get their attention. 'We want to know what you think,' he cried.

Michael Edgerton spoke up. 'I'll tell you what I think,' he said. 'I think it'd be a shame – a rotten shame – to close Frimly Prim. My great-granddad went to that school, and my grandma, and my mum and dad. It's sort of historic, if that's the right word.'

'Yes!' cried Vikki Dunn. 'It is the right word, and I've got another. Heritage. Frimly Prim's part of our heritage, my mum says. It's been here over a hundred years and everybody's been a kid there. Everybody remembers stuff that happened to them there.'

'And,' put in Peter Weeks, 'there's some famous people who have gone to Frimly Prim. There's Billy Oliver who got the VC in World War One, and Sandra Lawn who went to Oxford University and ended up as a professor, and Keith Fletcher who played for Fulham and Man. United. What would they think of their old school closing down?'

Nobody answered Peter's question, but Arnold Dobson said, 'My dad says there's some things more important than money and this is one of them.'

'There's another side to it though,' said Gillian Watson.

Smudge looked at her. 'What other side?'

'Well – if you occupy somewhere or go on strike or something like that, you're stopping people doing what they've a perfect right to do. I mean, Frimly Prim's a council school, right? It belongs to the council, so they can shut it if they want to. We only go there – it isn't ours.'

'Oh, yes it is!' cried Shaun Palmer. 'We pay for it with our taxes – or at least our parents do – so it's ours. We vote for the council and they're supposed to do what we want.'

There were several other contributions, and then Smudge held up a hand for silence. 'OK,' he said. 'We've heard arguments on both sides. Now let's have a vote on it. Hands up those in favour.'

A number of hands went up. Skeeter counted. 'Ten,' she said.

Smudge pulled a face. 'Those against.' No hands went up. Smudge looked at Matthew Pinkney. 'Your hand didn't go up either time,' he accused. 'Are you for us or against us?'

Pinko shook his head. 'I'm not against you, Smudge. I'm just not sure how it'd work out, that's all. I mean, we'd get in a lot of trouble, and it might not do any good anyway.'

Smudge looked at the other non-voters. 'Is that how you feel too?' The three nodded. 'OK,' he said. 'Take a couple of days. Think about it, only don't tell anyone, especially not The Hass. The rest of us'll start working out some details, and we'll meet here the same time Thursday. If you want to join us then, that'll be fine. If not, we'll just have to manage without you.' He shrugged. 'I guess that's it for now.'

The kids drifted away through the drizzle, talking in twos and threes. Matthew Pinkney paused for a moment, gazing at Smudge and Skeeter. 'You're serious, aren't you?' he said. 'You're really going to do it.'

Smudge nodded. 'You'd better believe it,' he said.

CHAPTER FOUR

Killing A Pig

Tuesday and Wednesday were busy days for Smudge and his friends. There was school work of course, and then at break-times they met to make plans. There was a lot to think about. They had to be careful not to arouse anybody's suspicions. Both Golly and Mrs Ball were famous for having sharp eyes, and one of them was always on duty in the playground at break, so meetings had to be brief, with somebody keeping watch. They talked about when they should occupy the school, and how. They discussed the sorts of things they would need if they were to live for days or even weeks inside the building: food, bedding and clothes. All these things would have to be smuggled into school without parents or teachers noticing. The more they thought about it, the more they realised how difficult it was going to be. And even if it all went right and they managed to lock themselves in with their supplies, what was to stop the adults just smashing the door in and chasing them all out again?

'What we need,' said Cher on Wednesday morning, 'is a hostage.'

'What for?' asked Smudge.

'To stop the grown-ups breaking in.'

'How would that work?'

Cher sighed. 'We tell 'em if anybody breaks in something awful will happen to the hostage.'

Smudge nodded. 'OK, but who?'

Cher grinned. 'Three guesses.'

Smudge frowned, deep in thought. 'I know!' cried Skeeter. 'The Hass, right?'

'Sssh!' Cher glanced round nervously. 'Keep your voice down, dummy – Ping-Pong's somewhere around.' Ping-Pong was Mrs Ball's nickname.

Smudge chuckled. 'I like it. I knew The Hass would come in handy one day.'

On Wednesday afternoons the juniors always went with Golly to the Almshouses to give the old people a hand. The Almshouses was a row of six ancient cottages where some of the oldest people in Frimly lived. They had a warden, who kept an eye on them in case anybody had a fall or was taken ill, but it was impossible for one person to do everything that needed doing, and that's where the children came in. They'd dig and weed gardens, paint and decorate, go to the mini-market or the launderette – there was always something the old folk needed a hand with. It had gone on for more years than anyone could remember, and most of the children looked forward to Wednesday afternoons.

Cher in particular liked to visit the Almshouses. Her great-grandma was one of the residents, and Cher would wash up the old lady's lunch things and make a cup of tea while they had a chat. On this particular Wednesday the old lady said, 'It's a shame, if you ask me.'

'What is, Gran?'

'The school, of course. Frimly Prim. Closing it.'

'Oh, yes.' Cher wanted to say, they won't close it – not if we can help it, but she didn't.

Their plan had to be a deadly secret, even from Gran.

'I went to that school myself, y'know. Seventy years ago.' The old lady smiled, remembering. 'Frimly Board School, it was then. My dad had to pay a penny a week for my lessons.' She looked at Cher. 'It's all right you smiling, young woman. A penny was a lot of money in them days. Took some finding.' She smiled to herself. 'Mr Waterhouse was Headmaster, and he were a terror. First thing in a morning he'd make us stand in a line, and do you know what he'd do?'

Cher, wiping a breakfast plate, shook her head. Old people have interesting stories to tell, and Cher liked listening to Gran.

'He'd walk along the line, very slowly, inspecting us. We'd hold our hands out and turn 'em over so he could see if they were clean. He'd look at our faces, clothes and clogs. If somebody's clogs weren't shining he'd say, "Have you cleaned your clogs this morning, so-and-so?" and if the answer was no, so-and-so got the cane.' The old lady chuckled. 'Eee – I remember one morning he stopped by Ebor Gummersall. Ebor were a farmer's lad and a proper little tearaway. Anyway, Mister Waterhouse stopped by him and said, "Have you cleaned your clogs this morning, Ebor?' and Ebor said, "Naw – has'ta cleaned thine?"' The old lady laughed wheezily, shaking her head.

'What happened to him?' asked Cher.

'Ooh, it was terrible, Cheryl. Terrible. Well, you didn't dare talk back in those days. Not like now. He got a terrific walloping from Mr Waterhouse, and when his father got to hear about it he got another one from him. He was a tearaway all right, but he was quiet for a long while after that.'

Cher pulled a face. 'I'm glad I wasn't a kid in those days. I'd have thought you'd be glad to see the place closed.'

'The old lady shook her head. 'It wasn't all inspection and punishment, love. We'd some happy times too.' She smiled. 'Harvest time, the Headmaster would close the school because all the children were needed in the fields. He'd close it for the day if someone was killing a pig, too.'

'Killing a pig? Why?'

'Because all the kids'd go to watch, love. There'd be nobody in school.'

'Ugh!' Cher wrinkled up her nose. 'Who wants to see a pig killed?'

Her gran laughed. 'Well, you see, there was no telly or anything like that. Nothing exciting to watch, so anything a bit different always drew a crowd.'

'Yuck.' Cher dried the last spoon and hung up the tea towel. 'So you don't want Frimly Prim to close, Gran?'

'Of course not, Cheryl. None of us do, here at the Almshouses. It's part of our lives, you see. We all went there as children. Doris Palmer next door went back and taught there. And anyway,' she chuckled, 'who'll keep the gardens tidy and run to the shops when all the children have gone?'

Cheryl looked at the old lady. 'Don't worry, Gran,' she said. 'It hasn't happened yet, and who knows – maybe it never will.'

CHAPTER FIVE

Plan of Action

Walking home that afternoon, Cher told Skeeter and Smudge about her conversation with her great-grandma. 'So you see,' she said, 'the old folks are on our side. They don't want the school to close.'

Skeeter looked at her. 'You didn't tell her what we're going to do?'

Cher shook her head. 'No, of course not. D'you think I'm stupid?'

Smudge shook his head. 'They might not be on our side once we occupy the place, Cher. Old people can be funny about things like that.'

'I think they'll support us,' said Cher. 'Gran will, anyway.'

Skeeter shrugged. 'Doesn't really matter, does it? I mean, they wouldn't be able to help or anything, would they? Most of 'em can hardly walk.'

Smudge pulled a face. 'You don't know

what they might do, and anyway, it's nice to
know somebody's on your side, even if they
don't actually do anything.'

When Smudge got home, Jilly was swinging
on the gate. She gave her brother a sly look.
'I know all about you,' she said.

'What d'you mean?' growled Smudge.

'School,' said Jilly. 'You're going to do
something.'

'No, I'm not.' His heart lurched but he

kept his voice calm. 'I don't know what you're talking about.'

Jilly smiled sweetly. 'Oh, yes, you do. You're going to try to stop them closing the school, and if you don't let me join in I'll tell Mum.'

'There's nothing to tell, and even if there was it wouldn't do you any good. We don't have infants in our gang.'

'I'm not an infant, I'm seven, and I can do anything your stupid gang can do.'

'Well, as it happens we're not doing anything, so you can just go and take a running jump at yourself.' He strode through the gateway and was halfway up the path when she called after him.

'I will join in, and if you won't let me I'll do it with some of my friends, so there.'

By afternoon break on Thursday their plans were complete. As far as they could tell, Jilly had said nothing to her mother and neither Golly nor Ping-Pong suspected anything, though Stanton Hassett was becoming curious. They were huddled in their usual corner when Skeeter spotted The Hass lurking nearby. She nudged Cher, who went, 'Sssh!' Smudge stopped talking and they all looked at the intruder.

'Is there something you're wanting, Hass?' asked Cher.

Stanton Hassett nodded sulkily. 'Yes, there is. I want to know what everybody's whispering about. Something's going on and if you don't tell me, I'll go to Mr Robertson.'

Cher stared at him. 'You do,' she said, 'and I'll push two fingers up your nose and pull your eyeball down.'

'You won't.'

'Try me.'

'Tell me what's happening.'

'Nothing's happening, but something'll happen to you if you don't shove off.'

'It's not fair. Everybody knows except me. I've seen 'em, whispering in little gangs. It's about me, isn't it?'

Smudge laughed. 'Is it heck. Who'd waste

time whispering about you, Hass? Are you going to shove off now, or do we get to play marbles with that eyeball?'

The Hass moved away. They followed him with their eyes. 'Sooner or later,' said Cher, 'someone's going to talk too loud and he's going to hear.'

Smudge nodded. 'Better warn everybody at the meeting this aft.'

It wasn't raining when school finished for the day and the juniors began making their way towards the quarry. The Hass was no problem after school because his folks lived in Bannerfield and his dad picked him up at the gate, so there were no spies around as Cher, Smudge and Skeeter faced the meeting.

'Right,' said Cher. 'We've all had a couple of days to think about it, and we've got a plan of action. When we were here on Monday, four people weren't sure about joining us. How do those four feel now?' Her eyes found Matthew Pinkney's. Pinko grinned and looked down. 'We'll join in,' he murmured. 'Won't we, guys?' The other three nodded. Cher grinned.

'Great. Well, the plan is to do it Monday lunch-time, when dinner's over. Golly'll have gone to the bank same as every Monday, and Ping-Pong will be in the yard with the infants. It should be dead easy for us to get ourselves inside the building and lock the door, but the hard bit will be getting our stuff in.' She looked around. 'Can everybody manage to smuggle a sleeping bag or blanket out of the house sometime this weekend?'

Everybody thought they could. Cher smiled. 'Good. And food. The more food we can take in, the longer we'll be able to last out. Can everybody bring food?'

Everybody said they'd bring food. 'Right,' said Cher. 'Smudge is going to tell you what to do with your stuff once you've got it out of the house.'

Smudge nodded. 'What we thought was, we'd hide everything near school, some-where where it'll be easy to grab when the time comes.' He looked at them. 'You all know the little brick shed on the edge of the field – the one they keep sports equipment and gardening stuff in?' There were nods and murmurs of assent. 'Well, that's the place. The football team plays away on Saturday and grass-cutting's over for this year, so nobody's likely to go in the shed. Sometime tomorrow, Skeeter will borrow the key from the office and unlock it. As I said, nobody's likely to check the door, so the chances are it'll be open all weekend. Now it's up to you to decide when to bring your stuff, but whenever you do it, be careful. Carry it inside something – a plastic bag or whatever. Don't let anybody see what you've got, and don't open the shed if there's a grown-up about.

'Oh, and I don't think we should talk about any of this at school from now on. The Hass is getting suspicious, and we don't want to put him on his guard or we'll have a tough job grabbing him on Monday. And talking about Monday, when I give the signal to go, don't mess about finding your own stuff. Just grab the bundle nearest to you and get it inside the school. There'll be plenty of time later to sort everything out. Has everybody got that?'

Everybody had. They sorted out the signal, and made sure somebody was bringing a tin-opener, a torch and a few other things they might need. It was all over by ten to four, and the kids slipped away to begin collecting their stuff. The three friends stood for a moment, watching the others depart. Cher took a deep breath. 'Well,' she said. 'That's it. No going back now.'

'No.' Smudge, hands in pockets, frowned. 'No going back.'

Skeeter hacked at a stone with the toe of her trainer. 'The siege is about to begin,' she murmured. 'The siege of Frimly Prim.'

CHAPTER SIX

Easy

It was easy. Far easier than Smudge had expected. By a quarter to one that Monday afternoon lunch was over. Golly's Micra pulled out of the staff car park at ten to, and at five to one Cher counted thirteen infants, including Jilly, following Ping-Pong on to the field. There should have been fourteen, but a quick check by Skeeter and Smudge showed no infant inside the building, so one must be away ill. At one o'clock precisely, Skeeter poked her head round the kitchen door and cried, 'Mrs Dean, Mrs Cockcroft – you're wanted in the yard – an accident – one of the infants!' The dinner ladies, both of whom had daughters in the infants, dropped their dish mops and ran. The building was empty.

Smudge stood on the top step. The juniors were pretending to play but he could feel their eyes on him. He raised his right

arm. Skeeter appeared behind him. 'OK,' she whispered. He dropped his arm. It was a minute after one.

Swiftly, the juniors abandoned their games and converged on the shed. Within twenty seconds its door was open and the first kids were hurrying across the yard with armfuls of food and blankets. On the step, Skeeter began counting them in while Smudge kept an eye on Ping-Pong. In the middle of the yard, Stanton Hassett stood gaping as his

classmates tottered by with their bundles like a column of ants. Cher ran across to him. 'Stanton!' she cried. 'Your dad's on the phone – wants to speak to you, urgently.'

'I bet he does,' muttered The Hass, following Cher towards the door. 'I don't know what's going on here, but Dad's obviously got wind of it.'

Smudge watched the field. The two dinner ladies had reached Mrs Ball. He couldn't hear their voices, but he could see that they were both talking to her at once, waving their arms and pointing towards the school. As he watched, Ping-Pong glanced towards the yard, saw that something was not quite right and began hurrying back across the field, hampered by the infants who clustered round her, vying with one another to hold her hand.

Smudge looked across the yard. The last kid was emerging from the shed. 'Come on!' he yelled. 'Hurry it up – we've been spotted.'

It was a close thing. As the hindmost junior bore his burden through the doorway, Mrs Ball reached the tarmac and came trotting towards the school. 'Rory!' she cried. 'Rory Smith – what on earth is going on in there?' She was no more than two metres away when Smudge stepped back, swung the door shut and shot the bolt.

Stanton Hassett was three steps inside the secretary's office when the door closed behind him and his arms were seized. He wriggled and kicked but it was no use. Matthew Pinkney and Arnold Dobson were two of the strongest boys in the school and they held him in an iron grip. 'Gerroff me!' he yelled. 'I'm wanted on the phone.'

'No, you're not,' grunted Pinko. 'That was a trick to get you in here. Take it easy now, or Dobsy and me'll pull your arm off and beat you to death with the soggy end.'

'What's happening – what you gonna do with me?'

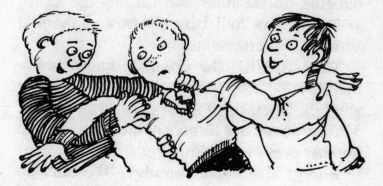

Pinko grinned. 'You're our hostage, Hass. You know what a hostage is, don't you?'

''Course I do. I'm not thick. But what's going on?'

'Never you mind.'

The door opened and Cher looked in. 'Got him?'

Pinko nodded. 'Easy-peasy. Can we kill him now. Cher?'

'Don't be silly. Take him to the juniors' and lock him in the stockroom, then go to the kitchen and help the kids pile stuff against the door. Hurry up.'

By the front door, Smudge and Skeeter were supervising the removal of food and bedding to the classrooms. On the other side of the door, Ping-Pong and the dinner ladies were beginning to get upset. They'd tried banging on the door and rattling the knob, and now Mrs Ball bent down and shouted through the letter slot.

'Rory Smith!' she cried. 'I know you're behind this silly prank, and it's gone far enough. Open the door at once, d'you hear?' You could see her fingers holding up the flap and her eyes peering in.

'Sorry, Miss,' said Smudge. 'We can't do

that. We're occupying the school.'

'You'll be occupying something else when Mr Robertson gets back,' cried the teacher.

Smudge wasn't sure what that meant, but it didn't sound good. 'Sorry, Miss,' he repeated. 'But we're not coming out till they promise to keep Frimly Prim open.'

He left the doorway and walked quickly through the school, checking that things were going according to plan. Every window was locked and guarded. In the kitchen they'd unplugged a fridge-freezer and shoved it against the door. In the two classrooms kids were sorting stuff out: stacking tins and jars and packets and laying out makeshift beds on the floors. From beyond the door of Golly's stockroom the voice of The Hass could be heard, listing the things his dad would do to his captors when he got hold of them. In the hall Sarah Cashman and Peter Weeks were working with felt-tips on big squares of card, making a sign to go in the window. 'WE LOVE FRIMLY PRIM!' it said.

So far, so good, thought Smudge. The building's ours, but goodness knows what happens next. All we can do is wait.

CHAPTER SEVEN

A Box of Chalks

It wasn't a long wait. At twenty past one Michael Edgerton, on guard at a front window, saw the Head's yellow Micra nosing through the gateway.

'Golly!' he cried.

Smudge nodded. 'Right. This is where the fun begins.' He ran out into the corridor and yelled, 'Stand by, everybody – Golly's back.' He turned. 'Skeeter?'

'Coming.' Skeeter emerged from the infants'. 'What's up, Smudge?'

'Golly'll try to get in,' he rapped. 'I think we can stop him if he can't see into the lobby, so we've got to block up the letter slot. Find some dusters or dish rags or something – anything – and block it up. I'll get The Hass.'

Skeeter ran towards the caretaker's room. Smudge went back into the juniors'. 'Mandy, give us a hand here, will you?' He unlocked the stockroom door. Stanton Hassett backed away.

'What you gonna do?' he squeaked. He might have tried charging past Smudge, but Amanda Tyrrell was blocking the doorway and she was a big strong girl.

'Nothing,' Smudge told him. 'As long as you behave yourself and do as I say. Come on.'

He grabbed The Hass's left hand, Mandy seized the other and they marched him out into the corridor. As they approached the lobby, Smudge said, 'Whatever I tell Golly, you back me up, right?'

'How d'you mean?'

'You'll see, Hass. One word out of place, and you'll eat a box of chalks.'

Skeeter had stuffed the letter slot with cloths and was nailing some strips of wood

across to keep them in place. 'Hey, brilliant!' cried Smudge. 'Where'd you find that stuff?'

'Lawson's room.' Mr Lawson was the caretaker.

'Great!'

As Skeeter stopped hammering, somebody outside started. A rain of blows shook the door and Golly's voice yelled, 'Smith! Rory Smith, open this door immediately or I'll have Mr Lawson break it down and have the bill for the damage sent to your father.'

'Sir!' cried Smudge. 'Don't do anything to the door. We've tied Stanton across it. If you break it down you'll pull him in two.'

There was silence for a moment. Smudge thought he could hear whispering. Then Golly called, 'Is this true, Stanton Hassett? Are you there?'

Mandy squeezed The Hass's arm and Smudge whispered, 'Chalks.'

'Y – yessir,' croaked The Hass. 'It don't half hurt, sir.'

There was another pause, then Golly said, 'I'll give everybody five minutes to think about the trouble Rory Smith is leading them into. If the door's still fastened then, it becomes a matter for the police.' There was the sound of footsteps retreating, then silence. Skeeter looked at Smudge and gulped.

'Oh, heck.' she said.

Smudge and Skeeter hung about in the lobby for a few minutes but nothing seemed to be happening so Skeeter said, 'You hang on here, Smudge, while I do the radio bit.' She sought out Vikki Dunn. 'Vikki, did you bring your radio like you said?'

Vikki nodded. 'It's there on Ping-Pong's table.'

'Great. We'll need it in a bit.'

'What for?' asked Shaun Palmer, who'd been carrying tins and packets of food to the kitchen.

'To hear what they say about us,' Skeeter told him.

'About us?' he gasped, but Skeeter was leaving the room.

She went to the office, lifted the receiver

and punched out the number she'd scrawled on a crumpled scrap of paper. There was some buzzing and a click and a voice said, 'Radio Bannerfield, can I help you?'

'Yes,' said Skeeter. 'I'm Sally Keith. I'm eleven, and I go to Frimly Primary School in Frimly. I'm there now. They want to close our school so we've occupied it. Sixteen of us. Seventeen if you count the hostage. Will you mention it on the news, please?'

It wasn't as easy as that, of course. The woman asked some questions, said, 'Hold a moment, please,' and went away. Skeeter held on. Through the office window she could see Golly and Mr Lawson in the doorway of the caretaker's house. As she watched, a police car swung into the yard and PC Wilde got out. There was some more noise down the phone, and the same voice said, 'Sorry to keep you waiting, caller. We're sending someone over. Thanks for letting us know. Bye.'

Skeeter returned to the lobby and told Smudge. He grinned. 'Wicked. There's nothing like publicity. It embarrasses 'em, my dad says.'

A knock on the door made them both

jump. 'We don't want any,' said Smudge. 'Go away.'

A man's voice answered. 'Less of your cheek, sunshine. I'm a police officer and I'm advising you to open this door.'

Smudge looked at Skeeter. 'Fetch The Hass,' he whispered. 'Quick. Get someone to help you.' Aloud he said, 'Sorry, Mr Wilde. Can't do that. We want our school, that's all.'

'This isn't the way to get it, lad. Come on, open up. Mr Robertson's sent for your parents.'

Oh, crikey. Smudge gulped. Dad'll love that, and Mum's gonna be highly delighted too, especially if they've called her from work. He pulled a face and said, 'We've a hostage tied to the door and someone's coming from the radio. You'd better leave us alone, Mr Wilde, or something terrible will happen.' He gulped, wondering how long Skeeter was going to be fetching The Hass; wishing he felt as brave as he was trying to sound.

CHAPTER EIGHT

Hass-Cream

Skeeter was back nearly straight away. She and Rebecca Weeks marched The Hass into the lobby just as Catherine Ingham came hurrying from the kitchen. 'Smudge!' she cried. 'They're rattling the door in there, trying to get in.'

Smudge grinned. 'What, with that freezer in front of it? No chance.'

'Someone keeps charging at it,' said Catherine. 'Every time he hits it, it bulges in.'

'Move some more stuff in front of it,' said Skeeter. 'And I'll try a trick I just thought up.'

She called through the door. 'Hey, can anybody hear me out there?' Nobody answered, but Skeeter continued anyway. 'Tell whoever it is that's charging the kitchen door that if he does it one more time our hostage goes in the freezer.'

There was still no reply, but a few moments later Catherine returned to report that the assault on the door had ceased. Smudge and Skeeter exchanged grins, but Stanton looked nervous.

'Hey, Skeeter?' he croaked. 'You wouldn't really put me in the freezer?'

'You bet I would. You'd be the world's biggest ice-lolly, Hass. They'd put you in *The Guinness Book of Records*.'

'Hass-cream!' cried Smudge, and everybody laughed except Stanton.

'You wait till my dad gets here,' he growled. 'You won't be laughing then.'

But it was Smudge's dad who arrived first. Peter Weeks, sticking up his notice in the juniors' window, saw him coming. 'Hey, Smudge!' he yelled. 'Your dad's here and I don't think he's come to buy you a Mars bar.'

Mr Smith marched straight up to the door. 'Rory?' he barked. 'Are you there?'

Smudge looked at Skeeter and gulped. 'Y—yes, Dad,' he stammered.

'Good, now listen. Open this door and I'll only stop your pocket money for six thousand weeks and strangle your hamster. Keep it locked and I'll pack you off to a boarding school I know of where there are no holidays, the Headmaster grows his own canes and they feed you on cold lumpy porridge with hairs in it.'

Smudge pulled a face at Skeeter, who whispered, 'Don't give in.'

'It's all right for you,' hissed Smudge. 'My dad's a terror when he's mad.'

The Hass smirked. 'Give in,' he mocked. 'Save an innocent hamster.'

'He doesn't mean it about my hamster,' murmured Smudge. 'He loves animals, my dad.' It was true, but Smudge felt like giving in anyway. The only thing that stopped him was the thought of what the kids would say if he cracked so easily.

He faced the door. 'I'm not coming out, Dad,' he said firmly. 'I can't let the others down.'

His father's reply was drowned out by the roar of a powerful engine and the squeal of brakes. The Hass looked towards the door, his face alight. 'That's Dad arriving,' he crowed. 'You've had it now, the lot of you.'

They thought he'd come banging on the door but he didn't. He disappeared inside the caretaker's house and a moment later the phone rang in the office. Cher pulled a face. 'Bet I know who that is,' she said. 'Are you going to get it, Smudge?'

Smudge shrugged. 'Expect so.' He went into the office and picked up the phone with a trembling hand. 'Frimly Prim,' he said. 'Smudge speaking.'

'Smudge?' spluttered the caller. 'Don't you dare use nicknames with me, boy.'

'OK, sir.'

'Where's my son, Smith? What're you doing to him?'

'D'you mean The Hass, sir? We're not doing anything to him. He's fine.'

'Put him on, then. I want to speak to him. And don't call him The Hass.'

'OK, sir. He can't come to the phone though. He's tied up right now.'

'Tied up? How d'you mean, tied up?'

'He's tied across the door, sir, so he'll sort of break in two if anybody opens it.'

There was silence for a moment. Smudge could hear Hassett senior breathing. Then he said, 'I'll tell you what you're going to do, boy.'

'What, sir?'

First, you're going to release my son and send him out.'

'The Hass, sir? Release The Hass?'

'I've warned you about nicknames, Smith.'

'I know, sir. Golly hates nicknames too, and so does Ping-Pong. Skeeter and Cher like 'em, though.' He could hear Ainsley Hassett grinding his teeth.

'You're going to be sorry for all this, Smith, I promise you.'

'Yes, sir.'

'So. You send out my son, and then you gather your little band of followers together and you come out of my restaur – I mean, out of that school, leaving everything as you found it. Any damage, and your father will pay. Any delay, and you're for the high jump. D'you understand?'

'All except one bit, sir.'

The Chairman of the Governors sighed. 'Which bit don't you understand, Smith?'

'That word you started to say, sir, instead of school. Rester-something. What was that, sir?'

'N-nothing. It was nothing. Slip of the tongue. Now – are you going to release my son and give up this ridiculous game, or do I put the whole thing in the hands of the police?'

'You can put the whole thing in the hands of Old Mother Hubbard,' said Smudge. 'We're keeping The Hass and we're staying put.' He slammed down the phone and remained for a time, leaning against the desk. He was shivering, and he felt as though he might be sick at any moment.

CHAPTER NINE

Goodies and Baddies

'Hey, Smudge.' Darren Waterhouse looked sheepish. Daniel Rawnsley and Gillian Watson didn't look too happy either.

'What's up?' asked Smudge, though he thought he could guess. He was sitting on the swivel chair in the office.

'Some of us have been thinking,' said Darren.

'Oh, yes?' Smudge fiddled with the cap of a ballpoint. 'What about?'

'About this. Us being in here and them out there. Golly. Mr Hassett. The police. Gillian's mum and dad just showed up. Nobody's on our side, are they, Smudge? Everybody's against us.'

Smudge looked at him. 'Did you think it would be easy, Daz?'

'Well, no, but –'

'Look. This is a fight, right? A fight to save our school. People get hurt in fights. If

58

you don't fancy it, why did you join us in the first place?'

'We didn't know it would be like this,' said Gillian. 'My mum's crying, Smudge. I've never seen her cry before.'

'It isn't just that,' said Darren. 'We're not sure we're right, you see. If we knew we were right it'd be different, but we don't.'

'Course we're right,' Smudge told him. 'We want our school. What's wrong with that?'

'Well, say this was a film on telly, right? If it was a film on telly and we were the goodies, those folks out there would be the

baddies, wouldn't they?'

Smudge shrugged. 'I guess so.'

'But they're not, are they? I mean, OK –
Ainsley Hassett might make a baddie, but
not Golly. Not PC Wilde. Not even the
council, really. They're just doing their job
and we're messing them about. We could be
the baddies, Smudge.'

'No, we couldn't!' flared Smudge. 'Well –
I don't think we could anyway.' He looked at
the three of them.

'D'you want to give in? Is that it?'

'Well, no – we don't want to, Smudge. It's
just . . .'

'Listen. Do you know what'll happen if
the three of you give up? Do you?'

Daniel looked at him. 'What?'

'Everybody else'll pack it in too. It'll be all
over in just –' He looked at his watch. 'Three
and a half hours. Not much of a fight, eh?'

'No, but –' The boy broke off as Catherine
Ingham burst in, her face alight. 'Hey,
Smudge – come quick! It's the old folks.
They've got flags and placards and they're
singing. Come and see.'

It was true. The old people from the
Almshouses – all except Flo Clapham who

couldn't walk – were there by the gate with home-made banners and boards. Even Vera Hassett was there and she was The Hass's gran. They were walking round and round in

a tight circle, the six of them, and they did seem to be singing.

'Open that window a bit,' said Smudge. 'Let's hear the words.'

They opened the window a fraction, keeping a sharp eye out for lurking adults. The words of the song came wafting across the twilit yard.

'Bannerfield Council is no use,
Squash 'em up for orange juice,
Ainsley Hassett is a fool,
Send him packing – Save Our School.'

Smudge turned to Darren Waterhouse. 'Hear that, Daz? Now tell me nobody's on our side.'

'Who's that woman near the old folks?' Cher pointed.

'That's Pippa Ripley from Radio Bannerfield,' cried Amanda. 'I've got a poster of her at home.'

'Yes,' chuckled Smudge. 'And that thing round her neck's a cassette recorder. She's recording the song. It'll be on radio.' He turned to the others, his eyes shining. 'We're gonna be famous,' he cried. 'We're gonna win!'

CHAPTER TEN

Getting Cold

It wasn't as easy as that, of course. After a while Pippa Ripley went away and the old folks stopped circling. They stopped singing too, but they didn't leave. They stood in a little knot by the gate, watching the school. If one of the kids waved through the window somebody would wave back, but it was getting dark and soon they could hardly see one another.

'Hey, Smudge,' said Pinko. 'Is it my imagination, or is it getting cold in here?'

'It's getting cold,' Smudge told him. 'And it'll get colder. The heating's on a time switch and it went off at four. What we need's some grub.' He looked around. 'Who's good at cooking?'

'My mum,' said Gillian mournfully.

Skeeter looked at her. 'Your mum's not here,' she rapped. 'Come on – who's gonna help me make a really enormous supper? I'm starving.'

'I'll come,' volunteered Shaun Palmer. 'My dad's a chef.'

'And me,' said Catherine. 'Mine's a pig.'

The three of them went off to the kitchen and before long a mixture of appetizing smells was making everybody's mouth water. Presently Skeeter yelled, 'Come and get it!' and they hurried along to the hall, leaving two kids by the window to watch the adults.

While the children tucked into sausages, beans and chips, the adults held a meeting in the caretaker's front room to decide what to do.

'I don't think we ought to break in,' said Ainsley Hassett. He'd have loved to break in really – smash the door down and drag that Rory Smith out by the scruff of the neck, the cheeky young wassock – but he was afraid something awful might happen to his son if they did.

PC Wilde agreed. 'The thing to do in sieges,' he said, 'is wait. They always surrender in the end, and that way nobody gets hurt and there's no damage to property.'

'That's all very well,' Mr Watson protested. 'But my wife's going frantic here. Our Gillian's not strong, you know. She's got a weak chest. Who knows what it'll do to her, spending the night in that cold, draughty school?'

'They've got bedding,' said the policeman. 'Sleeping bags and so on. And anyway, I doubt they'll spend the night. When it gets late and they're cold and frightened and starting to miss their mums, they'll come out. You see if they don't.' He looked at the group of parents. 'If I were you I'd go home, get some sleep. Mr Robertson and I will take turns keeping an eye on things, and as soon as the children come out we'll get them home. OK?'

And so it was agreed. As the children ate tinned fruit and custard for pudding, the parents slipped away, along with Ping-Pong and the dinner ladies. The old folks, cold and tired, went too; all except Alice Ward who had a secret plan. She lurked in the shadows by the bike shed, waiting for things to quieten down.

CHAPTER ELEVEN

A New Hostage

It was on the seven o'clock news. The kids had just finished clearing up after their meal. The dinner ladies' radio was playing in the kitchen. Radio Bannerfield News. Arnie Earnshaw reading it. 'Sssh!' went Skeeter,

turning up the volume. Everybody stopped rattling crockery. There was something about the government. Everybody groaned. Then the Middle East. More groans. Then Ireland. Then Frimly Prim.

'Pupils have barricaded themselves inside the primary school in the village of Frimly,' said Arnie Earnshaw. 'The school is threatened with closure, and the pupils are occupying the building in an attempt to persuade the council's Education Department to change its mind. A short time ago, our roving reporter Pippa Ripley spoke with parents, staff and governors outside the school.'

What followed was a bit crackly, but they heard Pippa Ripley talking with Golly, Ainsley Hassett, Mr and Mrs Watson and Alice Ward. When old Alice said, 'I think it's disgusting, closing our school without even asking us what we think about it,' everybody cheered. And when Ainsley Hassett got his words muddled and called himself the Gairman of Chuvenors they dropped two plates laughing.

When the item was over and everybody started talking at once, Smudge clapped his hands and said, 'Hey, listen!' They stopped talking. 'That's our second victory,' he said, 'and we've only been here six hours.'

'What was our first victory?' asked Vikki Dunn.

'Getting the old folks on our side,' Smudge told her. 'Tomorrow we'll be on TV. That'll be number three. Everybody will know about us, and the Education Department will be getting really worried. All we have to do is sit tight and not give up. We've got some lovely grub inside us, there's warm bedding and nobody's breaking the door down.' He grinned. 'There's no doubt about it, it's round one to us.'

'The infants'll be the girls' bedroom,' said Smudge. 'And the boys'll sleep in the juniors'.'

'It's not bedroom,' said Rebecca Weeks. 'Not when it's at school. It's dorm, short for dormitory. I know, because I've read a lot of books about boarding school.'

'OK,' said Smudge. 'The infants' is the girls' DORM and the juniors' is the boys' DORM. Satisfied?'

'Lovely,' smiled Rebecca, who'd always

longed to be a boarder.

They got the two rooms ready, but it was only eight o'clock and nobody felt like sleeping. 'I know,' said Michael Edgerton. 'Let's tell stories.'

They locked The Hass in the stockroom with his sleeping bag, posted guards at the doors and windows and everybody else gathered in the hall. They sat in a circle on the floor with blankets or sleeping bags draped round their shoulders.

'Turn all the lights off except one,' said Cher. 'It'll be like round the campfire.'

So they turned off most of the lights and Skeeter said, 'Who's first?'

'Me,' volunteered Peter Weeks. 'I've got a belter of a story. It's called, *The Haunted School*.'

'Oooh!' cried about ten voices. 'That's all we need.'

'Surely somebody knows a nice cheerful story?' said Skeeter.

'I do,' grinned Darren. '*The Classroom Murders*, it's called.'

'Oooh, shut up!' shivered Vikki. 'It's bad enough without that. I'll start crying for my mum in a minute.' Everybody laughed, and

suggestions started coming in thick and fast.

'*The Mad Caretaker.*'

'*Blood on the Stockroom Floor.*'

'*The Body in the PE cupboard.*'

'*The Frimly Prim Cannibal.*'

Everybody was laughing and squealing and making so much noise that nobody heard the knocking. Nobody except Sarah Cashman. She screamed.

'What the heck's up with you?' Sarah's scream had made everybody jump. There was no laughter now.

'Sssh!' Sarah scowled. 'Something knocked.'

'S-something?' Arnold Dobson turned pale. 'What sort of something?'

'I don't know, do I? Listen – there it goes again.'

'It's the door,' said Cher. 'Somebody's at the door, that's all.'

'You answer it then,' croaked Sarah. 'I'm not.'

'Chicken!' Cher got up.

'Want me to come with you?' asked Smudge. Cher shook her head.

'Well, be careful. Don't open it. Ask who it is and what they want.'

'You don't have to tell me,' said Cher. She left the circle and tiptoed into the lobby. As she reached the door there was another volley of knocks. 'Hello?' called Cher. 'Who's there?'

'The Big Bad Wolf.' Cher thought she recognised the voice.

'Gran?' she cried. 'Is that you?'

'Yes, it's me. Open the door.'

'Are you by yourself?'

'Of course I am. You don't think I'm on their side, do you? Come on – open up before they come out of the caretaker's house.'

Cher drew back the bolts and unlocked the door.

Alice Ward stepped over the threshold. 'Shut it quick, love – they might be watching.'

Cher locked the door, then looked at the old lady. 'What d'you want, Gran – you should be in bed long ago.'

'I'm your new hostage, Cheryl.'

Cher gaped. 'What d'you mean?'

'What I say. I'm your new hostage. You can let young Stanton go, and then his dad won't be such a nuisance to you'.

They walked across the dark lobby. 'What are you all up to, anyway?'

Cher chuckled. 'We were scaring one another with stories. Your knock gave half of us heart attacks.'

'I've got a story for you,' said the old lady. 'It's about your Chairman of the Governors.'

Cher looked at her. 'Ainsley Hassett? What sort of story, Gran?'

'The sort that'll get him off your backs, I should think,' said her great-gran. 'If you threaten to give it to the papers and the telly and all that.' They'd reached the hall. 'Let me get comfy in your story circle, and I'll start at the beginning.'

CHAPTER TWELVE

Teddy Bears

'Once upon a time,' said Alice Ward, 'before he became a husband and a father and a rich man and a very important Gairman of Chuvenors, Ainsley Hassett was a schoolboy. He attended Frimly Primary School, and he was a villain.'

'A villain?' gasped Skeeter. 'How d'you know?'

'His mum told me.'

'What sort of villain?' asked Smudge. 'What did he do?'

'Oooh,' the old lady shook her head. 'It'd be quicker to tell you what he didn't do, but we've got all night, so here goes.'

'Do you know what a protection racket is?' She peered round the circle over the top of her glasses, but nobody knew. 'Well,' she said. 'I'll tell you. To run a protection racket you need a gang, and Ainsley Hassett had one. What he'd do was, he'd pick on some small boy or girl, or someone who was a bit timid, and he'd say, "Give me twenty pence a week and my gang will protect you – stop people beating you up." And the victim would say, "Oh, but I'm all right, Ainsley, thank you. Nobody's beating me up." And then Ainsley would say, "Somebody will, if you don't cough up the twenty pence," and the victim would say "Who?" And Ainsley would laugh his nasty laugh and say, "My gang, of course."'

'That's awful,' cried Gillian. 'Did he do that to a lot of people?'

'Oh, yes. There must have been ten, fifteen children paying him twenty pence a week. And that wasn't all.'

Smudge looked at her. 'He did other things as well?'

'Oh, yes. There was book duty for one thing. Children paid Ainsley three pence each time they borrowed a book from the school library. If they didn't, he and his gang would tear the book or drop it in the mud and the borrower would get into trouble. Then there was lavatory charge. If you needed the loo at playtime you paid three pence or the gang wouldn't let you in. There was a crossing toll as well: two pence to cross with the crossing lady. If you crossed somewhere else you could get knocked down or a teacher might see you. And then there was a cloakroom fee. A penny a day to hang your coat up. If you didn't pay, you'd find your coat torn or scribbled on with felt tip, or perhaps it would be gone.'

Pinko whistled. 'That's amazing, Mrs Ward. How did he get away with it?'

The old lady smiled. 'He didn't, Matthew. Not for ever. One day a teacher caught him tearing somebody's library book and the whole story came out.'

'What happened?' gasped Skeeter. 'Did he go to prison?'

'No,' chuckled Alice Ward. 'But he thought he was going. What they did was, they sent for his parents, and they decided the best thing to do was to scare young Ainsley really badly so he wouldn't dare do anything of the sort again. Well – he'd been making umpteen pounds a week from his various rackets. So they got the local bobby in and sent for Ainsley, and when he saw the policeman he nearly had a fit. He thought they'd send him away for life. The bobby gave him a terrific telling off – they say you could hear him shouting half a mile away – and that night he got a belting from his dad. So it never came out – he didn't have to go to court or anything so only a handful of people knew about it and most of them have died or gone away. But it's all written down in the school logbook, which is in the office somewhere, and if I were you I'd find it and let him know you've got it and pretend you're thinking of giving it to the newspapers or the telly.' She smiled. 'I think he'll leave you alone then. He might even change sides. It's all his idea you know, closing the school.'

'His idea?' Cher gaped. 'But he's a school governor.'

The old lady nodded. 'I know, but he's what's known as a property developer as well, and he wants to convert this place into a posh restaurant. He's even got a name picked out, his mother says: The Old School House Restaurant.'

'Oooh!' cried Skeeter. 'No wonder you called him a villain, Mrs Ward. He still is, if you ask me.'

The old lady smiled. 'People don't change, Sally. Not really. Anyway, if somebody'll get me a nice cup of tea, I'll tell you what I think you should do next.'

Everybody felt better with Alice there. It was like having your gran nearby. They got a good night's rest, and when they woke at dawn the old lady had breakfast ready.

When they'd eaten and cleared away it was time to put Alice's plan into operation. Smudge had found the logbook. He'd found four, in fact, with entries going back to World War Two, but it hadn't taken long to

find the right one: 1968. That was the year, and it was all on one page, so Cher made a photocopy of it while Smudge told The Hass he was being released.

'Giving in, are you?' sneered Stanton. 'After just one night?'

'No way,' Smudge replied. 'We've got a better hostage, and you've got a message to deliver.'

'A message? What message?'

'This.' Smudge held out a brown envelope which contained the photocopy.

'Give this to your dad and watch his face when he opens it.'

They let him out. PC Wilde was standing at the door of the caretaker's house, but Smudge had the door open and shut before he could move. After that they could only wait, passing the time by rolling up their bedding and stacking it in corners.

At half-past eight Michael Edgerton, keeping watch at the juniors' window, called out, 'Hey, everybody – a van's just pulled up with BBC TV on it.' Everbody rushed to look. It was true. Five people got out of the van and began unloading equipment. In a few minutes they had a camera set up and a

woman was talking to PC Wilde while a man held a microphone which was fluffy and looked like a Yorkshire Terrier on a stick.

'Fame!' yelled Smudge. 'The whole world can see us now.' They opened some windows, cheering and waving when the camera swung round to film them. 'Hey, Mandy,' cried Skeeter. 'Go and put the telly on, see if we're on live.'

They weren't, but things were happening in the yard. The old folks appeared again with their placards. There was a new one. It said, FREE ALICE WARD – SAVE OUR SCHOOL. The TV people abandoned PC Wilde and started filming them. They'd just got the camera focused on the old folks when something even more interesting happened. Children's voices were heard singing, and as Smudge and the others goggled in disbelief, a line of infants swung into the yard with Jilly at their head. There were ten of them, and each one was clutching a teddy bear. They were singing *The Teddy Bears' Picnic*, and Jilly had a placard. TEDDIES FOR FRIMLY PRIM, it read. They marched into the middle of the yard and sat down in a circle, cuddling their teddies and singing lustily. The camera swung to cover them, and the reporter squatted down to speak to Jilly while the fluffy mike hovered above her head.

'Hey, Smudge,' laughed Cher. 'I thought you said that sister of yours was too small to help us?'

Smudge shrugged, grinning. 'I take it all back. She's brilliant. Look at those telly guys lapping it up.'

The woman was still talking to Jilly when the door of the caretaker's house opened and Ainsley Hassett appeared, looking pale, with The Hass at his heels. He hurried to his car, ducking under the microphone and pushing aside the woman who had leapt up and was trying to interview him. The kids in the window cheered as the Hassetts got into the vehicle, and ten teddies waved it off as it swung out of the yard in a cloud of exhaust.

Alice Ward smiled. 'He's off to Bannerfield,' she said. 'To see some men about a school.'

They watched the road for the rest of the morning but the Hassetts didn't return. Round about lunch-time a cold wind started to blow and the sky clouded over. The infants, bored and uncomfortable, got up and drifted away, dangling their teddies. The knot of old folks stamped their feet and propped their placards against the wall so they could rub their hands together.

'Nasty weather on the way,' said Alice. 'Could be cold in here tonight.'

'We'll manage,' grinned Skeeter. 'Take more than cold to make us give up now.'

Smudge was in the kitchen helping with

lunch when the TV people approached the building, so it was left to Cher and Skeeter to shout into the fluffy mike which was thrust at an open window.

'How long are you prepared to stay in there?' yelled the woman.

'Forever, if we have to,' cried Cher.

'What about food?'

'There's plenty.'

'You're holding an old lady hostage. Do you think that's fair?'

'She's my great-gran,' shouted Cher. 'I wouldn't do anything to hurt her. She's fine.'

'Do you think you'll win?'

'We know we will. When will we see ourselves on the telly?'

'Watch the one o'clock news. What about all the worry you're causing your parents?'

'What worry?' cried Skeeter. 'They know where we are, which is more than they know most of the time.'

'OK. Thanks for talking to us.' The mike was withdrawn. The crew retreated to their van. It was sleeting.

By the time lunch was over the van had gone and the yard was deserted. The wind was blowing sleet in rattling volleys against the windows. The old folks had gone home to thaw out while Golly, PC Wilde and several parents sat drinking mugs of scalding tea in Mr Lawson's front room.

At one o'clock everybody gathered round the TV and there it all was: the school with Peter's notice and their faces in the windows, Jilly and her friends with their teddies, the old folks with their placards, Ainsley Hassett scurrying to his car. Best of all, there was a bit at the end they hadn't been expecting, where the woman said that education chiefs and governors were meeting at that moment to discuss the situation.

'They're going to give in!' crowed Smudge. 'You just see if they don't.'

CHAPTER THIRTEEN

The Right Thing

Nothing else happened that afternoon, except that the weather got worse. The wind swooped and racketed round the building like something trying to get in and drifts of soggy sleet accumulated in corners. They watched themselves on the six o'clock news, and the weather forecast which followed it promised more of the same. It was, said the weatherman, unusually cold for October.

And old Alice was right. After the heating went off at four o'clock the temperature plummeted. It was as though the wind was

sucking all warmth out of the school. The leaden sky made darkness come early, too, and by seven o'clock the children were huddled in the hall, wrapped in bedding. They tried telling stories but it was too uncomfortable. At half-past seven Smudge said, 'This is no good. We're just getting frozen. We might as well go to bed.'

'That's the best place on a night like this,' agreed the old lady.

'This'll be our last night anyway,' said Skeeter.

She was right, but it didn't happen they way they all expected.

It had taken Cher ages to drop off, and it seemed to her that she hadn't been asleep two minutes when something woke her. She propped herself on one elbow, knuckling her eyes. Her right hip felt sore from the hard floor. She'd been woken by a noise, and as she peered at her watch it came again. It was a voice. A loud, tinny voice. She couldn't make out the words but she recognised the sound. Somebody was speaking through a loud-hailer.

Oh, crikey! She remembered stuff she'd

seen on telly – police surrounding the gangsters' hide-out, warning them through loud-hailers, then storming the building with tear gas and guns. She found her trainers, pulled them on and, with the laces trailing, began groping her way towards the juniors'.

In the juniors', several boys were already awake. Somebody was shining a blinding light at the window and the voice was clearer here – you could make out some of the words. Smudge saw Cher.

'What's the time?' he mumbled.

'Twenty-past two,' Cher told him. 'What's happening? Are they breaking in or what?'

'Dunno.' Smudge was tugging on a shoe. 'There was a siren a while ago – like a fire engine or a cop car, and then this voice, something about the Almshouses, I think.'

They were making their way towards the window, screwing up their eyes against the glare and stumbling over boys and bedding, when there came a thunderous knocking on the main door. 'They're breaking in!' cried Skeeter, who'd followed Cher. 'I'll tell 'em we've got old Alice tied to the door.'

She ran down the corridor and through

the lobby. The knocking hadn't stopped.

'Listen!' she yelled. 'Our hostage is tied to that door. Break in and you'll pull her apart.'

The knocking stopped and a voice called, 'Sally Keith – is that you?' Golly's voice. Skeeter gulped. 'Yes sir, it's me.'

'Well, listen, Sally. There's an emergency at the Almshouses – a gas leak. There's a build-up of gas which might explode at any moment. They've evacuated the residents but it's a terrible night and we need to get them under cover immediately or they'll die. We need the school, Sally.'

While Golly had been speaking, Cher, Smudge and a few of the others had arrived in the lobby. Skeeter looked at Smudge.

'What do we do?' she whispered.

Smudge shook his head. 'Dunno. Could be a trick.'

'They wouldn't do that, would they?' said Cher.

Golly called. 'Sally? Are you still there?'

'Yes, sir.' Skeeter sounded as though she might cry.

'What's up?' Alice Ward had entered the lobby. 'What's all the racket about?' Quickly, Cher told her what Golly had said.

'D'you think its a trick, Gran?'

The old lady shook her head. 'I don't know, Cheryl. The gas fittings in the Almshouses are very old, but I'm not sure whether it's a trick. You'll have to decide between yourselves what to do.'

'After all that.' Smudge's voice cracked. 'We were winning. It was nearly over, and now . . .' he looked around. All the children were in the lobby. 'What d'you think?'

'We've no choice, Smudge,' said Mandy. 'We've got to open up.' Several voices

muttered in agreement. Smudge wiped his cheek with the back of his hand. 'OK,' he said. 'If that's how it's got to be.'

Swiftly, he and Skeeter drew back the bolts and turned the key. The door opened. 'Thank you,' gasped Golly. 'Believe me, you've done the right thing.' He turned and called to somebody outside as the wind blew a whirl of sleet into the lobby. Two fire fighters appeared, supporting old Flo Clapham between them. She was in her nightie, and somebody had thrown a blanket round her shoulders.

Smudge turned to the children. 'Quick,' he said. 'Gather up the sleeping bags and make six good beds, get some water boiling for tea.'

More fire fighters clomped in with shocked and shivering old folks. Golly sent Mr Lawson to turn on the heat, then went into the office and made some phone calls. By twenty to three the old people, swathed in bedding, were drinking hot tea, and parents, sleepy but relieved, had begun arriving to take their children home. The siege of Frimly Prim was over.

CHAPTER FOURTEEN

Three Cheers

That was Tuesday night. Wednesday there was no school because the old folks didn't leave till lunch-time, and because Golly knew the children would sleep and sleep, so it was Thursday morning when Smudge, Cher and Skeeter met outside the shop. Smudge had Jilly with him but he didn't seem to mind.

'Hi, Smudge, Skeeter,' grinned Cher. 'Hello, Jilly. How are you feeling?'

'Fed up,' growled Smudge. 'We'd have won if it hadn't been for that rotten gas leak. I know we would.'

'Yes, well. That's how it goes, as my mum would say.'

'We had to let the old folks in, didn't we?' said Skeeter. 'I mean, they'd helped us with their placards and stuff, and your great-gran was terrific, Cher.'

'I know. She'll be just as cheesed off as we are.'

They didn't usually have assembly on Thursdays, but Ping-Pong came into the cloakroom at ten to nine and told everybody to gather in the hall.

'I thought so,' muttered Smudge. 'He's going to give us big trouble because of the siege. You see if he doesn't.'

They lined up in the hall. Ping-Pong closed the door and stood in front of it. Golly mounted the platform, looking serious.

'He's going to suspend us,' whispered Smudge. 'Look at his face.'

'Children,' said Golly. 'I have two items of news for you, one sad, one happy. First the sad news, which is that our Mr Hassett has decided to resign as Chairman of the Governors. He and his family are leaving the district, which means that your friend Stanton won't be coming to school any more.'

'That's the sort of sad news I like,' hissed Cher, and Smudge and Skeeter giggled. By the door, Ping-Pong cleared her throat in warning.

'And now, the happy news.' Smudge

looked at Golly and saw that he was smiling. 'Hey,' he whispered. 'Surely it's not – it can't be . . .'

'Sssh!' hissed Skeeter. 'Listen.'

'At a meeting on Tuesday, the Education Department decided that it won't be closing our school after all.'

'Yippee!' screeched Smudge. He couldn't help it. The infants turned to see who'd made such a dreadful noise in assembly. Golly glared down at him.

'What did you say, Rory Smith?' he rapped.

'I said – I meant . . .' Smudge could hardly speak for laughing. Or was he crying? He couldn't tell.

'Er – um – come on then – three cheers for Frimly Prim!' he cried, and the children cheered so loudly that their voices went soaring over the village to the Almshouses where the old folks heard, and knew.